ISRAEL

COUNTRIES IN CRISIS

ALAN WACHTEL

Rourke Publishing

Jefferson Madison
Regional Library
Charlottesville, Virginia
WITHDRAWN

30408 2629

R

© 2009 Rourke Publishing LLC

All rights reserved. No part of this book may be reproduced or utilized in any form or by any means, electronic or mechanical including photocopying, recording, or by any information storage and retrieval system without permission in writing from the publisher.

www.rourkepublishing.com

PHOTO CREDITS: AFP/Getty Images: p. 18; Steven Allen/istock: pp. 13, 21; Nicolas Asfouri/AFP/Getty Images: p. 39; AWAD/AFP/Getty Images: p. 36; Esaias Baitel/AFP/Getty Images: pp. 32-33; Corbis: pp. 9, 16; Gabriel Duval/AFP/Getty Images: pp. 26-27; Limor Edrey/AFP/Getty Images: pp. 4-5; Getty Images: pp. 6-7, 20, 23, 24, 29, 30; Tom Hahn/istock: p. 37; Atta Kenare/AFP/Getty Images: 42; Saul Loeb/AFP/Getty Images: p. 41; Moti Meriri/istock: p.12; Vadim Onishchenko/istock: p. 38; Noel Powell/istock: p. 11; UN photo/Yutaka Nagata: p. 25; U.S. Department of Defense: p. 40.

Cover picture shows Israelis celebrating Jerusalem Day, May 2007. Israel captured East Jerusalem during the Six-Day War in 1967. Many countries do not recognize Israel's claim over this territory. [Getty Images]

Produced for Rourke Publishing by Discovery Books
Editor: Gill Humphrey
Designer: Keith Williams
Map: Stefan Chabluk
Photo researcher: Rachel Tisdale

Library of Congress Cataloging-in-Publication Data

Wachtel, Alan, 1968-
    Israel / Alan Wachtel.
        p. cm. -- (Countries in crisis)
    Includes index.
    ISBN 978-1-60472-350-2
    1. Arab-Israeli conflict--1993---Juvenile literature.
                Israel--Juvenile literature.
    DS126.5 .W25 2009
    956.94 22

                                2008025139

Printed in the USA

CONTENTS

CHAPTER ONE

THE CRISIS TODAY

On September 11, 2007, a rocket fired from Gaza crashed into an Israeli army base. The young soldiers on the base were lucky. The rocket hit an empty tent. No one was killed, but **shrapnel** from the rocket injured 40 Israeli soldiers sleeping in nearby tents. Some were badly hurt.

The rocket was fired from Gaza. Gaza is a Palestinian-Arab area that borders Israel. Today, Gaza is controlled by Hamas. Hamas is a group that wants Palestinian Arabs to have their own country. It believes that Israel should not exist. After the rocket attack, a speaker from Hamas said, "We consider this a victory from God

Israeli police officers look at a damaged building in the town of Sderot. The building was hit by a Palestinian rocket on May 26, 2007.

for the resistance."

Many Palestinian rockets are shot into Israel. Most of them do no harm, but they are a constant threat. Israel's army patrols its border looking for Palestinians about to fire rockets. In August 2007, Israeli soldiers saw people touch a rocket launcher in a field. The soldiers fired at them. Later, they discovered they had killed three children. Israel says it works hard to prevent tragedies like this, but it also says it must stop the Palestinian rocket attacks.

Israel has been a country in crisis for as long as it has existed. Over the last twenty-five years Israel's most urgent conflict has been with the Palestinian Arabs who live in Gaza and the West Bank. These are disputed territories that border Israel and are mainly occupied by Palestinians, but also

by some Jewish settlers.

In spite of the recent violence, things looked up for Israel and the

A bus full of Palestinians just released from prison in Israel arrives in the West Bank in December 2007. The prisoners who were freed were members of Fatah, the Palestinian party led by Mahmoud Abbas.

Palestinians in the fall of 2007. Ehud Olmert, Israel's prime minister, and Mahmoud Abbas, the leader of an important Palestinian group called Fatah, were getting ready to meet for peace talks. Before the talks, Israel released almost 100 Palestinian prisoners.

THE ISRAELI-PALESTINIAN CONFLICT:

The Israeli-Palestinian conflict is not simple. Growing numbers of Jews began moving to Palestine in the 1800s. The **United Nations (UN)** divided Palestine after World War II to create a homeland for the Jewish people.

The Palestinians are an Arab group that live in the same region as Israel. The UN tried to create a country for them, too, but they rejected the idea of having two countries in Palestine. When Israel was founded in 1948, many Palestinian Arabs thought Israel took land that should have been theirs. Some Palestinian Arabs also did not want a Jewish country in Palestine.

Israelis and Palestinians have met for peace talks many times. Sometimes the talks make a little progress, but they have not come close to ending the conflict. Fighting between the two sides never seems far away. In addition to the rockets that are often shot into Israel, Palestinian suicide bombers have **terrorized** Israelis. In response to these attacks and the rockets, Israel's army often raids Palestinian land. Israel has also built a huge barrier to protect its people from Palestinian attacks. It is not all-out war, but it is constant conflict. To many people, the Israeli-Palestinian conflict is one

PALESTINE'S HOLY SITES

Jerusalem, the present capital of Israel, is home to the holiest sites in Palestine. Most Israelis are Jews. The Temple Mount, for Jews, is holy because it was the location of the First and Second Temples. The Western Wall of the Temple Mount is the holiest site in Judaism. Many Jews pray at the Wall. For Muslims, and most Palestinians are Muslim, the Dome of the Rock and the al-Aqsa Mosque are sacred. They believe that Muhammad rose to heaven from the spot that the Dome of the Rock marks. The Dome of the Rock is built on the Temple Mount.

Jewish man prays at the Western Wall (also called the Wailing Wall). The Wall is one of the most sacred sites in Judaism.

of the world's biggest problems.

CHAPTER TWO

TROUBLE FROM THE START

Israel is a small country in the part of the Middle East called Palestine. Around 6.5 million people live there. Modern Israel borders Lebanon and Syria to the north, Jordan and the West Bank to the east, and Egypt and the Gaza Strip to the west. Its coastline runs along the Mediterranean Sea. Most of Israel's people and big cities are in this region. The climate here is temperate. In the south of the country is the Negev Desert, which is hot and dry. South of the desert is the Gulf of Aqaba. In the east the Dead Sea marks the lowest point on Earth.

WHERE IS ISRAEL?

LEBANON
Golan Heights
SYRIA
Nahariyya
Har Meron
Haifa
Mediterranean Sea
Nazareth
Hadera
Netanya
Nablus
WEST BANK
Jordan River
Tel Aviv
Rishon Le Ziyyon
Ramallah
JERUSALEM
Gaza • Sderot
GAZA STRIP
Judean Desert
Dead Sea
ISRAEL
Negev Desert
JORDAN
EGYPT
Sinai
EUROPE
ASIA
AFRICA
ISRAEL is in the Middle East
Gulf of Aqaba

The ruins of Masada, the fortress in the Judean Desert that was built by King Herod. Herod was the pro-Roman king of Judea from 37 BC to 4 BC.

Palestine has a long history going back to prehistoric times. Ancient peoples began farming in the area around 4,000 BC From 3,000 BC the area was inhabited by Semites, including the Israelites who spoke Hebrew. The ancient Hebrews founded Judaism there. In the following centuries, Palestine was conquered by the Assyrians, the Babylonians, the Persians, and the Greeks.

By the first century AD the Romans ruled the region. When the Jews rebelled against Rome, the Romans invaded the town of Jerusalem and destroyed Jerusalem's Jewish temple. The Jews, forced into exile, began migrating to North Africa and Europe.

Over the centuries, Arabs and Turks also ruled the region. For the Jews that left their homeland there were frequent battles against **persecution**.

Toward the end of the 1800s, some Jews in Europe decided they needed a homeland where they

Jerusalem today has both ancient and modern buildings. The gold-domed al-Aqsa Mosque is built on the Temple Mount.

A plate of Middle Eastern food, including hummus and falafel balls.

FOOD IN ISRAEL

The food people eat in Israel reflects the diversity of the country's culture. Eastern European Jews introduced foods such as gefilte fish, which is made from chopped fish and spices. Middle Eastern and North African foods, such as falafel and hummus, are also popular.

would not be persecuted. Palestine, they decided, was the best place for their country. Jerusalem, was the ancient home of the Jews. In the biblical era, a fortress called Zion stood in Jerusalem. The movement to set up a Jewish country in Palestine became known as Zionism.

A small Jewish community had always lived in Palestine, but from the 1800s Jews from Europe had begun moving to Palestine. They bought land, farmed, and mostly lived in peace with the local Arabs. Between 1882 and 1914, there were two big waves of Jewish **immigration** to Palestine. By 1914, about 90,000 Jews lived in Palestine, along with many more Arabs.

During this time, Palestine was ruled by the **Ottoman Empire**. Some Arab leaders did not like having so many Jewish immigrants in Palestine. They wanted the Ottomans to stop Jewish immigration. In 1914, however, World War I broke out. By the time the war ended in 1918 the Ottoman Empire had fallen and Britain and France took control of the region.

AFTER WORLD WAR I

Britain was in charge of an area called the British **Mandate** of Palestine. It included the land of modern Israel and Jordan, as well as the West Bank and the Gaza Strip. Some British officials supported Zionism. During the war, in 1917, Britain issued the Balfour Declaration. The Balfour Declaration said that Britain would work to create "a national home for the Jewish people" in Palestine. Britain had also talked to Arab leaders, trying to get their help against the Ottomans. One thing they discussed was independence for the Arabs.

In 1921, Britain split Jordan off from the Mandate. With the remaining land, Britain tried to create a single country with Jews and Arabs as citizens.

THE PROBLEMS WITH PARTITION

"Partition means that neither will get all it wants. It means that the Arabs must acquiesce [accept] in the exclusion from their sovereignty of a piece of territory, long occupied and once ruled by them. It means the Jews must be content with less than the Land of Israel they once ruled and have hoped to rule again. But it seems to us possible that both parties will come to realize that the drawbacks of Partition are outweighed by its advantages.

The British recommendations on the partition of Palestine, from the Peel White Paper June 22, 1937."

No one liked this plan. Fighting broke out with Arabs against Jews, and everyone against the British. By 1937, Britain gave up the idea of creating one country. It suggested creating separate Jewish and Arab countries, while keeping Jerusalem under British control.

WORLD WAR II AND BEYOND

Before a plan could be made, World War II began. All of Europe was threatened by Nazi Germany, led by Adolf Hitler. Knowing that Hitler was viciously **anti-Semitic**, Jews from Palestine joined Britain in fighting the Nazis.

Starved prisoners in a concentration camp in Austria, 1945. Millions of Jews died in these camps during World War II.

They also worked to bring as many European Jews as they could to Palestine. On the other hand, the Grand Mufti of Jerusalem, one of the most powerful Palestinian Arab leaders, sided with the Nazis.

The murder of millions of European Jews in the Holocaust made the Jews even surer that they needed a country of their own. After the war, supporting the Nazis hurt the Palestinian Arabs' cause in the eyes of Britain. Britain also questioned its support of a Jewish state because of attacks by the

DEIR YASSIN

One of the most notorious events of the Palestine Civil War was the Deir Yassin massacre. On April 9, 1948, members of the Irgun and Lehi killed many Palestinians in the village of Deir Yassin. Some say that the killings at Deir Yassin were intended to scare Palestinian Arabs off their land.

Irgun and Lehi, extremist groups that attacked British targets. Many thought the Irgun and Lehi were terrorists. More and more, Britain just wanted to get out of Palestine.

In early1947, Britain passed the problem of Palestine to the United Nations (UN) and said it would pull out of Palestine by May 15, 1948. By November, the UN voted to partition (split) Palestine into two countries, one Jewish and one Arab, with Jerusalem run by the UN. The Jews accepted this plan, but the Arabs did not.

ISRAEL'S WAR OF INDEPENDENCE

Fighting between Jews and Arabs in Palestine began after the UN vote. Neither had much of an army and both sides fought hard, but the Jewish forces were better trained than their enemies. During this time, Jews began defending the borders of what was to be their land, as well as Jewish settlements outside of the borders. This fighting is often called the Palestine **Civil War**.

When the British left, the Jewish state of Israel declared independence.

Israel's first prime minister, David Ben-Gurion, stands to deliver the country's Declaration of Independence on May 14, 1948. The portrait above him shows Theodore Hertzl, one of the first Zionists.

DECLARATION OF INDEPENDENCE

> [Israel] will be open for Jewish immigration. . . . it will guarantee freedom of religion, conscience, language, education, and culture. . . .it will safeguard the Holy Places of all religions.

Extract from the Declaration of Independence speech by David Ben-Gurion, May 14, 1948.

PALESTINIAN REFUGEES

About 700,000–750,000 Palestinian Arabs left their land just before and during the Israeli War of Independence. Most of them ended up as refugees in the Gaza Strip, the West Bank, Jordan, Lebanon, and Syria. This was the beginning of the world's biggest refugee crisis.

Immediately the U.S. and the **Soviet Union** recognized the new country. However, Israel's neighbors Egypt, Jordan, Syria, Lebanon, and Iraq responded by invading it. This war is known as both Israel's War of Independence and as the First Arab-Israeli War.

The new country fought for its life, and won. As in their battles with the Palestinians, the Israelis defeated the invading armies mainly because they were better trained, well organized, and well

Israeli soldiers hold an Iraqi flag captured during Israel's War of Independence.

ISRAEL'S ECONOMY

Agriculture has always been important in Israel. Among its main crops are citrus fruits, such as oranges. Vegetables are grown for local use and for export. Today, technology is a big industry in Israel especially in areas such as communications, computers, and aviation. Unlike many countries in the Middle East, Israel has no oil.

Jaffa oranges were one of the new country's top exports after 1948. Toward the end of the twentieth century however, orange cultivation declined.

motivated.

It also helped Israel that its enemies did not work together or trust each other. The new country gained its independence, but this fight was only the first of many.

CHAPTER THREE

THE ARAB-ISRAELI WARS

By 1949, the new country gained more land than it would have had under the UN plan. The Palestinian Arabs were even further from having their own country than they were before the war. Egypt and Jordan had taken over all the land not occupied by Israel.

Although the major fighting had stopped, Israel and its enemies did not sign peace treaties. Many people expected all-out war to quickly erupt again, but before it did, Israel changed. Between 1948 and 1951, its population grew to over 1.3 million. Its new citizens were Jews from around the world, especially Europe and the Middle East. The new country also developed its economy and military. By the mid-1950s, Israel was still small, but it was not weak.

1956: THE SUEZ CRISIS

Tensions rose between Israel and Egypt when Egypt blockaded the Strait of Tiran. Israeli ships needed to get through this crossing. Egypt had also angered Britain and France by taking control of the Suez Canal. Britain, France, and Israel made a plan. Israel would send its forces into Egypt's Sinai Peninsula, which bordered the Suez region. Britain and France would then send their forces to break up the conflict. Israel succeeded in reopening the Strait of Tiran, but Britain and France failed to regain control of the Suez Canal.

1967: THE SIX-DAY WAR

Any illusion of peace between Israel and its neighbors was shattered in 1967. After years of growing tension and failed **diplomacy**, Israel and its Arab neighbors again moved toward all-out war. Battles took place between Israel and Jordan and Syria. Egypt moved troops into the Sinai Peninsula, which borders

A family of Jewish immigrants sits outside their tent in Israel on December 1, 1949. Early immigrants to the new country were called pioneers.

Israel. It also again blockaded the Strait of Tiran. When Jordan and Egypt signed a defense agreement, Israel was surrounded.

Israel did not wait to be attacked. On June 5, 1967, it launched a **preemptive** strike.

Israeli tanks prepare for battle in the Six-Day War.

Within the first hours, Israel crippled Egypt's air force. Then, Israel took on its enemies' ground forces. By June 11, when the last cease-fire agreement was signed, Israel had taken the Sinai Peninsula and the Gaza Strip from Egypt, the West Bank from Jordan, and the Golan Heights from Syria. This short, shocking war became known as the Six-Day War.

1973: THE YOM KIPPUR WAR

If 1967 was a tough year for Israel, the early 1970s turned out to be even tougher. Diplomatic **negotiations** with the Arab countries had stopped. Palestinian terrorists killed eleven Israeli athletes at the 1972 Olympics in Munich, Germany. Egypt's army

UN RESOLUTION 242

After the Six-Day War, the UN passed Resolution 242. The Resolution calls for peace in the Middle East. Israel, Egypt, and Jordan all agreed to it, but it took many years for them to make progress toward peace. One problem was that the countries disagreed about how to interpret the words of the resolution.

was receiving weapons from the Soviet Union. In spite of all this, Israel's leaders believed their country had grown so strong that the Arab countries would not attack it.

They were wrong. On October 6, 1973, armies from Egypt and Syria fought their way into land controlled by Israel. Israel was taken by surprise. Not only were the Arab armies well trained and well armed this time, they launched their attack on Yom Kippur—an important Jewish holiday when most Jews would be praying, not thinking of war.

The members of the United Nations Security Council all voted for a resolution calling for peace in the Middle East on November 22, 1967.

Israeli soldiers cover their ears as they fire at Syrian forces in the Golan Heights during the Yom Kippur War.

THE PLO

In 1964, the Palestine Liberation Organization (PLO) was formed. This group was intended as a government for Palestinian Arabs as they worked toward a country of their own. It also included a military wing that attacked Israel. In the 1970s, the PLO became known for its terrorist tactics.

The Syrian army pushed into the part of the Golan Heights occupied by Israel. Egypt's army crossed into Israel-controlled Sinai. It took a few days for Israel to get its forces ready to fight back. The fighting was fierce. Egypt got more weapons from the Soviet Union, and Israel got more weapons from the United States. By October 10, Israel pushed the Syrian army back into Syria. About one week later, Israel's army had the Egyptian army surrounded. It was a stunning victory.

CHAPTER FOUR

PEACE AND TERROR

In 1976, Jimmy Carter was elected president of the United States. One of Carter's main goals was to work for peace in the Middle East. The U.S. president invited Israel's prime minister, Menachem Begin, and Egypt's president, Anwar Sadat, to a meeting at Camp David, in Maryland, in 1978. Begin wanted a peace treaty to prevent future wars. He also wanted Israel to keep occupied land that it

PEACE WITH JUSTICE

"In all sincerity I tell you we welcome you among us with full security and safety. This is in itself a tremendous turning point, one of the landmarks of a decisive historical change. We used to reject you. . . .
Yet I tell you, and declare it to the whole world, that we accept to live with you in permanent peace based on justice. We do not want to encircle you or be encircled ourselves by destructive missiles ready for launching, nor by the shells of grudges and hatreds.

From Anwar Sadat's "Peace With Justice" speech, November 20, 1977."

Egyptian president Anwar Sadat (left), U.S. president Jimmy Carter (center), and Israeli prime minister Menachem Begin (right) celebrate after signing the Camp David Accords on September 18, 1978.

needed for defense. Sadat, who no longer believed that Egypt could defeat Israel, mainly worked to get the Sinai Peninsula back. The talks were tense. In the end, Sadat signed a peace treaty with Israel, and Israel pulled out of the Sinai Peninsula.

With the most powerful Arab country at peace with Israel, the small country's neighbors were never again able to gang up on it. Israel and Jordan signed a peace treaty in 1994. Israel and Syria have never made peace, and Israel still occupies the Golan Heights.

ISRAELI SETTLEMENTS

More and more Jewish settlements were built in the West Bank and the Gaza Strip during the 1970s. By 1977, there were 31 Jewish settlements in the West Bank and 5 in the Gaza Strip. Some Jews believe that God wanted them to have this land, and they think settling in these areas will help to bring the messiah. Palestinians feel a lot of resentment toward Jews living in the settlements.

Israeli prime minister Menachem Begin (right, in white shirt) supports Jewish settlers as they establish a settlement in the occupied West Bank in 1974.

THE PLO AND LEBANON

To many Arabs, especially Palestinians, Egypt's treaty with Israel was a betrayal. Sadat paid for the treaty with his life: he was assassinated in 1982. As the crisis of Israel's wars with its neighbors was ending, a new crisis was about to explode.

Israel and the PLO had become bitter enemies. The PLO did not recognize Israel's right to exist. Israel viewed the PLO as a terrorist group. The PLO was based in Lebanon, and it had grown powerful. While Israel and Egypt were making peace, the PLO began attacking Israel more.

To fight the PLO, Israel invaded Lebanon in 1982. The Israeli army drove the PLO out of Lebanon, but the people and cities of Lebanon suffered greatly. Many people, even some Israelis, thought Israel fought too hard. Israel also let some of its Lebanese supporters massacre hundreds of Palestinians in the Sabra and Shatila refugee camps.

POSSIBLE PEACE

Israel's conflict with the Palestinians grew more complicated in the 1980s. Many small Palestinian groups carried out terrorist attacks. Unrest and poverty troubled the refugee camps and parts of the occupied territories of the West Bank and Gaza Strip. In 1987, the West Bank and Gaza erupted in an **intifada**. Violence filled the streets as Palestinians rebelled against the Israeli army.

The intifada lasted until the early 1990s, when Israel and the PLO signed the Oslo Accords in 1993.

HAMAS

Hamas was founded in 1987. Its charter says the group "strives to raise the banner of Allah over every inch of Palestine. . . ."

THE 1994 NOBEL PEACE PRIZE

Yasser Arafat, the leader of the PLO, and Yitzhak Rabin and Shimon Peres, Israel's prime minister and foreign minister, shared the Nobel Peace Prize in 1994 for their work on the Oslo Accords.

In this agreement, the PLO recognized Israel's right to exist and Israel recognized the PLO as the representative of the Palestinians. The two sides also worked for more self-government for the Palestinians in the occupied territories.

It was a time of hope. Many people thought peace was not far away. Some Palestinians, however, still refused to recognize Israel, and some Israelis opposed the government's policies. Hamas, a Palestinian **Islamist** group, struck Israel with many terrorist attacks. In 1995, a Jewish extremist assassinated

Israeli prime minister Yitzhak Rabin. The hope for peace faded fast.

Masked Palestinian protesters in the West Bank throw rocks at Israeli soldiers during the first intifada.

CHAPTER FIVE

THE SECOND INTIFADA

With the help of U.S. president Bill Clinton, new peace talks between Israel's prime minister Ehud Barak and Yasser Arafat took place in July 2000. Barak was serious about peace and the creation of a Palestinian state.

He offered the Palestinians all of the Gaza Strip and 92 percent of the West Bank. He also offered them a capital in part of Jerusalem. Almost everyone was shocked when Arafat refused the offer and walked out on the

U.S. president Bill Clinton (center) sitting with Israeli president Ehud Barak (left), and Palestinian leader Yasser Arafat (right), at Camp David in July 2000.

FAILURE AT CAMP DAVID

> " After 14 days of intensive negotiations between Israelis and Palestinians, I have concluded with regret that they will not be able to reach an agreement at this time. As I explained on the eve of the summit, success was far from guaranteed—given the historical, religious, political, and emotional dimensions of the conflict.
>
> *From Bill Clinton's Statement on the Middle East Peace Talks at Camp David on July 25, 2000.* "

talks. Arafat insisted that Israel withdraw to its 1967 borders and allow the return to Israel of all the Palestinian refugees and their children. These were conditions to which Israel would never agree. Some said Arafat did not really want peace.

CONTROVERSY OVER THE "RIGHT OF RETURN"

Israel will not allow Palestinian refugees and their families into the country because there are so many of them. Letting them in would make it impossible for Israel to keep a Jewish majority. Israel is a **democratic** country, unlike many other Middle-East nations.

SHARON VISITS THE TEMPLE MOUNT

In September 2000, Ariel Sharon, an Israeli leader, visited the Temple Mount. The Palestinians hated Sharon. They thought he could have stopped the massacres at Sabra and Shatila. Palestinians demonstrated against Sharon. The demonstrations grew into violent conflict with Israeli troops. The violence then grew into the second intifada, and it was more deadly than the first. Many Palestinian suicide bombers struck Israeli civilians, and Israel's army responded with fierce raids on Palestinian towns.

As the violence continued, Sharon was elected as Israel's new prime minister in February 2001. He surprised many people by coming up with two new ideas about how Israel should deal with the Palestinians.

Surrounded by security staff, Israeli leader Ariel Sharon visits the Temple Mount and al-Aqsa Mosque in September 2000.

Female soldiers of the Israeli army march through the Old City of Jerusalem. Women have always played an important role in the Israeli military.

THE WALL AND WITHDRAWAL

Sharon saw that Israel could not control the Palestinians and the occupied territories. He also saw that Arafat could not, either. First, he said that Israel should build a giant barrier between Israel and the West Bank. Then Israel should pull its forces and its settlers out of both the Gaza Strip and part of the West Bank.

A section of Israel's security wall in Jerusalem. The barrier was put up to protect Israelis from Palestinian terrorist attacks.

The barrier would prevent Palestinian terrorists from attacking Israelis. Pulling out

An Israeli girl watches her mother pack their belongings. They were among 8,000 Israeli settlers forced to leave their homes in Gaza in 2005.

ISRAELI VS. ISRAELI

Israeli settlers in the Gaza Strip and the West Bank were heartbroken by Sharon's plan. In 2006, Israeli soldiers forced the settlers to leave their homes. Israeli soldiers also removed Israeli settlers from the Sinai Peninsula in the early 1980s.

from the occupied territories would force the Palestinians to govern themselves. In 2006, however, Sharon became too sick to lead Israel. Ehud Olmert, the new prime minister, followed through with his plans.

CHAPTER SIX

A CRISIS WITHOUT END?

Hezbollah is an Islamist group that formed in Lebanon in 1988 to fight Israel's occupation of southern Lebanon. Today, it is a powerful political party in Lebanon. In July 2006, Hezbollah fighters crossed from Lebanon into Israel, killed eight Israeli soldiers, and took two hostages. Israel responded with furious airstrikes and a ground invasion. Prime Minister Olmert declared that Israel would destroy Hezbollah. Hezbollah, however, turned out to be stronger than Israel thought. The destruction in Lebanon reminded many people of the 1982 war. Hezbollah fired rockets into Israel, hitting the city of Haifa hard. After a month of fighting, both sides claimed victory even though it was clear Israel had not succeeded in destroying Hezbollah.

Israeli bombs strike Beirut, the capital of Lebanon, during the war between Israel and Hezbollah in the summer of 2006.

Israeli prime minister Ehud Olmert (right) and Palestinian Authority president Mahmoud Abbas (left) shake hands. The two leaders met for talks in Annapolis, Maryland, in November 2007.

HAMAS VS. FATAH

After Israel pulled out of the West Bank and the Gaza Strip, the Palestinians held elections. To the surprise of many, Hamas won a great deal of power. Fatah, the party of Arafat and Mahmoud Abbas, lost. This was bad news for Israel because Hamas opposes Israel's existence. Hamas and Fatah supporters then began fighting each other. By 2007, Hamas had control of the Gaza Strip, and Fatah had control of the West Bank. Israel placed tight sanctions on the Gaza Strip to try to get Palestinians to rebel against Hamas. Life in the Gaza Strip became grim, with much poverty and violence.

PEACE TALKS IN 2007

As Olmert and Abbas prepared for peace talks in November 2007, they faced many challenges. First, Abbas does not have much real power. Many international leaders attended the talks, but Hamas was completely against them. During the talks, Olmert and Abbas agreed to work toward a treaty in 2008, but they did not say what problems the treaty would address.

Meanwhile, supporters of Hamas held a big protest to show that they were against the talks. Without support from the majority of Palestinians it is not clear what changes Abbas can bring about. Israel may not be willing to make promises to a leader who does not have much power.

Secondly, many Israelis are against giving up more of the West Bank, a key Palestinian demand. Israeli settlers who live on this land would lose their homes. Some also believe that pulling out of the West Bank will make Israel less safe. The future for Israelis, and Palestinians living in the region is still a troubled one.

Iranian president Mahmoud Ahmadinejad delivers an anti-Israel speech in October 2000.

THE THREAT FROM IRAN

Many people believe that Iran is a threat to Israel. Iran's president, Mahmoud Ahmadinejad, has made speeches against Israel. Iran is developing nuclear technology. If Iran gets close to making nuclear weapons, some believe Israel may attack it.

TIMELINE

BC

ca. 10000 Hunter-gatherers are living in the region.

ca. 3000 Walled towns are built throughout the region.

ca. 2000 Birth of Abraham, a prophet of Judaism, Christianity, and Islam.

588 Kingdom of Judaea is taken over by the Assyrians; many Jews are deported to the city of Babylon (present-day Iraq).

300 BC-AD 400 Much of the Middle East is controlled by the Greek and then Roman Empires.

AD

70 Expulsion of Jews from Judaea by the Romans. Many Jews migrate to North Africa and Europe. This migration becomes known as the Diaspora.

313 Roman Emperor Constantine becomes a Christian, marking the beginning of the spread of Christianity.

600s Islam spreads throughout the Middle East and North Africa.

800-1914 Jews are migrating back to Palestine.

1948 Israel declares independence; first Arab-Israeli war.

1956 Suez War

1967 Six-Day War

1969-1970 War of Attrition

1972 Palestinian terrorists kill 11 Israeli athletes at Munich Olympics.

1973 Yom Kippur War

1977 Egyptian president Anwar el-Sadat visits Israel.

1978 Sadat and Menachem Begin sign Camp David Accords.

1982 Israel invades Lebanon.

1987 First intifada begins.

1994 Jordan-Israel peace treaty signed.

1995 Israeli prime minister Yitzhak Rabin assassinated.

2000 Arafat walks out on Camp David summit; second intifada begins.

2001 Ariel Sharon elected prime minister of Israel.

2004 Yasser Arafat dies; Mahmoud Abbas takes office.

2005 Israel withdraws from West Bank and Gaza Strip.

2006 Sharon suffers a stroke and retires; Ehud Olmert becomes prime minister; Hamas wins Palestinian elections; Israel battles Hezbollah in Lebanon.

2007 Violence between Hamas and Fatah in West Bank and Gaza Strip; summit between Ehud Olmert and Mahmoud Abbas.

ISRAEL

GEOGRAPHY

Area: 8,019 square miles (20,770 sq km)

Borders: Egypt, Gaza Strip, Jordan, Lebanon, Syria, West Bank

Terrain: Low coastal plain in the west, desert in the south, rugged hills in the north, and in the east the Dead Sea—the lowest point on Earth's surface

Highest point: Har Meron 3,963 feet (1,208 meters)

Resources: Timber, potash, copper ore, natural gas, phosphate rock, magnesium bromide

SOCIETY

Population (2007): 6,426,679

Ethnic groups: Jewish 76.4%, Non-Jewish (mostly Arab) 23.6%

Languages: Hebrew (official language); Arabic; English

Literacy: 97%

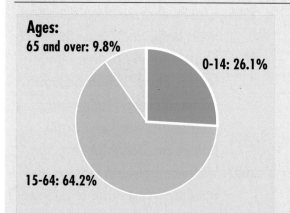

Ages:
65 and over: 9.8%
0-14: 26.1%
15-64: 64.2%

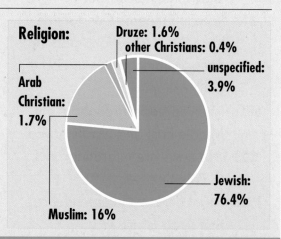

Religion:
Druze: 1.6%
other Christians: 0.4%
Arab Christian: 1.7%
unspecified: 3.9%
Jewish: 76.4%
Muslim: 16%

GOVERNMENT

Type: Parliamentary democracy   **Capital**: Jerusalem   **States**: 6

Independence: May 14, 1948

Law: Mixture of English common law, British Mandate regulations, and Jewish, Christian, and Muslim legal systems

Vote: Universal—18 years of age

System: President (chief of state elected for seven-year term); prime minister (elected every four years); 120-seat unicameral Knesset elected by popular vote every four years

ECONOMY

Currency: New Israeli shekel   **Labor force (2006):** 2.81 million

Total value of goods and services (2006): $170.3 billion

Poverty: 21.6% of the population below poverty line

Main industries: technology, wood, and paper products, potash and phosphates, food, tobacco, cement, metal products, chemical products, plastics, diamond cutting, and textiles

Foreign debt (2006): $83.01 billion

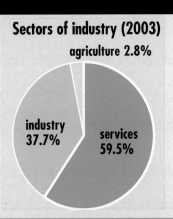

Sectors of industry (2003)

agriculture 2.8%

industry 37.7%

services 59.5%

COMMUNICATIONS AND MEDIA

Telephones (2006): 3 million fixed line; 8.4 million mobile

Internet users (2006): 1.9 million   **TV stations:** 17

Newspapers: about 20 daily papers and 4 national weeklies. Published mainly in Hebrew, but also in Arabic, English, and Russian   **Radio:** 3 stations

Airports: 53   **Railroads:** 533 miles (853 km)   **Roads:** 10,840 miles (17,446 km)

Ships: 18 over 1,000 tons   **Ports:** Ashdod, Elat, Hadera, Haifa

MILITARY

Branches: Army, navy, air force   **Service:** compulsory military service for Jews at 17 years of age—3 years for men, 2 years for women

GLOSSARY

anti-Semitic (AN-te se-MI-tik): unfriendly or hostile toward Jews

civil war (SIV-il-wor): war between members of the same country

democratic (dem-uh-KRAT-ik): having a government that allows the people to vote for their leaders

diplomacy (dip-PLOH-muh-see): talking between countries to solve problems

immigration (IM-uh-gra-shuhn): moving from one country to another

intifada (in-ti-FAH-dah): Arabic for *shaking off*, a Palestinian rebellion

Islamist (ISS-lulm-ist): working for government according to the rules of the religion of Islam

mandate (MAN-date): an area of land in which a conquering country is responsible for setting up a new government

negotiations (ni-GOH-shee-ay-shuns): talking with the goal of making an agreement

Ottoman Empire (OT-to-mun EM-pire): the Turkish empire that ruled the Middle East before World War I

persecution (PUR-suh-kyoo-shuhn): harmed because of religion, race, or beliefs

preemptive (pre-EMP-tiv): done to prevent a future problem

shrapnel (SHRAP-nuhl): pieces of a bomb

Soviet Union (SOH-vee-et YOON-yuhn): the communist superpower made up of Russia and fifteen smaller countries that lasted from 1922 to 1991

terrorized (TER-uh-rized): scared by attacks meant to cause political change

United Nations (UN) (yoo-NI-tid NAY-shuhns): the organization of countries set up after World War II to work for peace

FURTHER INFORMATION

WEBSITES

CIA Factbook

https://www.cia.gov/library/publications/
the-world factbook/geos/is.html

A store of facts and statistics on Israel.

BBC News Special Reports: Israel and the Palestinians

news.bbc.co.uk/1/hi/in_depth/middle_
east/2001/israel_and_the_palestinians/

A selection of news items about the Arab-Israeli conflict, including a timeline, voices from the conflict, and a feature on Jerusalem's holy sites.

Economist.com Country Briefings: Israel

www.economist.com/countries/Israel/

News and comments on business and economics in Israel. Includes country profile, background material, surveys, currency converter and web resources.

The Israel Museum, Jerusalem

www.imj.org.il

This website from the Israel Museum has information on ancient and contemporary art in Jerusalem. It also has online exhibitions.

BOOKS

Israel in the News: Past, Present, and Future. (Middle East Nations in the News (series). David Aretha. Myreportlinks.com, 2006.

Israel. Enchantment of the World (series). Martin Hintz. Children's Press, 2006.

Ehud Olmert: Prime Minister of Israel. Newsmakers (series). Michael A Sommers. Rosen Publishing, 2007.

Focus on Israel. World in Focus (series). Alex Woolf. Gareth Stevens Publishing, 2007.

INDEX

APR 2009

APR   2009